Daily Life THEN and NOW

Therese Shea

REAL LIFE readers™

Rosen Classroom™
New York

today

long ago

People wear hats.

One hat is from today.

One hat is from long ago.

How are they different?

People play games.
One game is from today.
One game is from long ago.
How are they different?

today

long ago

People ride bikes.

One bike is from today.

One bike is from long ago.

How are they different?

today

long ago

People wear shoes.

Two shoes are from today.

Two shoes are from long ago.

How are they different?

Look at these schools.

Which is from long ago?

DAILY LIFE
Long Ago
Today

Words to Know

bike

game

hat

school

shoes